Roller-coaster fun!

I grabbed Elizabeth's hand as our little car reached the top of the hill. We stopped there for a moment and then rushed down the other side.

Elizabeth and I screamed. It was just as scary as a big roller coaster in an amusement park!

"Ya-hoo!" Steven hooted.

We went up and down a few hills and around a big turn. Then we rolled back to where we had started.

"That was fun!" Elizabeth exclaimed.

"Can we go again?" I asked George.

"Of course," George said. "This is your roller coaster. You can ride it as much as you like."

Bantam Books in the SWEET VALLEY KIDS series

SWEET VALLEY KIDS

A ROLLER COASTER FOR THE TWINS!

Written by
Molly Mia Stewart

Created by
FRANCINE PASCAL

Illustrated by
Ying-Hwa Hu

BANTAM BOOKS
NEW YORK • TORONTO • LONDON • SYDNEY • AUCKLAND

To Oliver Chase

RL 2, 005-008

A ROLLER COASTER FOR THE TWINS!
A Bantam Book / December 1996

*Sweet Valley High® and Sweet Valley Kids® are
registered trademarks of Francine Pascal.*

Conceived by Francine Pascal.

*Produced by Daniel Weiss Associates, Inc.
33 West 17th Street
New York, NY 10011.*

Cover art by Susan Tang.

ISBN: 0-553-48334-X

Published simultaneously in the United States and Canada

*Bantam Books are published by Bantam Books, a division of Bantam
Doubleday Dell Publishing Group, Inc. Its trademark, consisting of the
words "Bantam Books" and the portrayal of a rooster, is Registered in the
U.S. Patent and Trademark Office and in other countries. Marca
Registrada. Bantam Books, 1540 Broadway, New York, New York 10036.*

PRINTED IN THE UNITED STATES OF AMERICA

OPM   0 9 8 7 6 5 4 3 2 1

CHAPTER 1

A Terrific Surprise

"**D**id I tell you about our vacation to Fantasy Forest?" I asked Amy Sutton. We were eating lunch in the school cafeteria with a bunch of our friends.

"Yes, Jessica," Amy told me. "Twice."

"The Enchanted Castle was really cool," I said. "Elizabeth and I met a boy who actually *lives* inside it. His name is Billy Grant."

"We know all about Billy!" Lila Fowler rolled her eyes. "His parents own Fantasy Forest. He gets to go on any of the rides whenever he wants.

He's the luckiest kid in America! You've told us about him at least a hundred times."

"More like a million times," Eva Simpson said with a giggle.

"A million times *today*," Ellen Riteman added.

Everyone laughed at that. Even my twin sister, Elizabeth.

My face got hot and red. I didn't understand what was so funny. When I first told my friends about our trip, they thought it was really interesting. Why were they laughing at me now?

"Don't get mad, Jess," Elizabeth said. "Ellen was just joking."

Don't get mad? How could Elizabeth say something like that? Of course I was mad!

Elizabeth and I are so different that sometimes I can't believe we are identical twins. But we are. Elizabeth and I are both seven years old. We have the exact same birthday. And we look just like each other. I have the same blue-green eyes as Elizabeth's. We both have long blond hair with bangs.

We are the only twins in Mrs. Otis's second-grade class at Sweet Valley Elementary School. I like school because I see all of my friends there. My best friends (besides Elizabeth) are Ellen Riteman and Lila Fowler. We play together at recess and pass notes during class. Mrs. Otis doesn't like it when we pass notes.

Neither does Elizabeth. She likes to pay attention and learn. She even likes to do her homework. Not me! Elizabeth's best friends are Amy Sutton and Todd Wilkins. They like homework too. Yuck!

Lots of people think that twins are totally alike. But just because we look the same doesn't mean we *are* the same. Still, Elizabeth and I share a lot of things, like the vacation we took to Fantasy Forest. It was the best *ever!*

"Did I tell you about the Princess Pageant?" I asked.

"Yes!" Eva said.

I tried to think of something that happened at Fantasy Forest that I *hadn't* told my friends about yet.

But before I could think of anything, Lila butted in. "Guess what?" she said. "Dad told me I could have a sleep-over pool party!"

"Cool!" Ellen said.

"Dad said I could have as many people as I like," Lila bragged.

"I'll help you plan it," Ellen offered.

"OK!" Lila agreed. "Do you want to help, Jessica?"

"No!" I said. I was mad at Lila for interrupting me. Why does she always have to be the center of attention?

* * *

4

"Do you think Mom and Dad would let us have a party?" I asked Elizabeth after school. We were at home, putting together a jigsaw puzzle. Our baby-sitter, Molly, was doing the sky. That's the hardest part.

"Maybe," Elizabeth said. "But Lila would get mad if we had one too. And her party would be fancier than ours."

Lila's dad is the richest person in Sweet Valley. He spoils her rotten. She is so lucky.

"If Lila is already having a party, why would you want to have one?" Molly asked me.

"Because Lila gets too much attention," I said.

"But she's your friend," Molly pointed out.

"I know," I said in a crabby voice.

Molly winked at me. "You shouldn't compete with your best friend."

"Why not?" I asked.

Before Molly could answer, I heard a really loud horn blow outside.

"What was that?" Elizabeth asked.

I jumped up. "Let's find out!"

Elizabeth, Molly, and I ran outside.

A huge truck was parked in front of our house. I'd seen trucks that big on the highway. But I'd never seen one on our street before. It looked weird.

Three men jumped out of the truck. They were wearing blue work suits with Fantasy Forest printed on the back.

"Is this the Wakefields' house?" one of the men asked.

"Yes!" I told him.

"May I help you?" Molly asked politely.

"We've got a present from Billy Grant for Elizabeth, Jessica, and Steven Wakefield," the man said. Steven is our big brother.

"What is it?" I asked.

The man smiled at me. "Your very own roller coaster!"

CHAPTER 2

The Wakester

Elizabeth and I jumped up and down and screamed for joy.

"Our own roller coaster!" Elizabeth said. "This is amazing!"

"I can't believe Mom and Dad didn't tell us!" I exclaimed.

"Me neither!" Elizabeth said.

"Me neither . . ." Molly looked thoughtful. "Do you think your parents knew the roller coaster was coming?"

"Of course they knew!" I said.

"Billy's parents wouldn't send us a roller coaster without asking Mom

and Dad first," Elizabeth said.

"Probably not," Molly said.

One of the workmen grinned at Molly. "It's going to take a while to put this thing together. Can we get started?"

"I guess that would be OK," Molly said.

"Where do you want it?" the workman asked me and Elizabeth.

"How about in the backyard?" Elizabeth suggested.

"OK," the workman replied. He opened the back doors of the truck. The workmen started pulling out big pieces of metal and bringing them into our backyard. Elizabeth, Molly, and I sat on the grass behind the house and watched.

Suddenly Steven ran into the backyard. His friends Bob and Joe followed him.

"What's going on?" Steven yelled.

"They're putting together our roller coaster," Elizabeth told him like it was the most normal thing in the world.

Steven's mouth dropped open. So did Joe's. And Bob's.

Elizabeth giggled. "Billy sent it to us," she said.

"Did *you* know it was coming?" Molly asked Steven.

"No," Steven said. "This is so cool!"

"Your very own roller coaster," Bob said. "You should give it a cool name like Steven's Scream Scene."

"Or Psycho Steven's Supersonic Spacecraft to the Sun," Joe added.

Steven grinned and turned to Joe. "Not bad!"

"No fair!" I shouted. "It's my roller coaster too."

"And mine," Elizabeth said.

"Maybe you could all come up with a name with Wakefield in it," Molly suggested.

"Hmmm." Joe frowned. "Ws are hard. And not too much rhymes with Wakefield. How about 'the Wakester'?"

"That sounds neat!" Molly said.

"I like it too," Elizabeth said.

I thought that Jessica's Cosmic Capsule would be a better name. But I didn't get to speak up because Lila, Eva, Ellen, and Amy came running into our yard.

"Hi!" Amy said. Her face was red from running. "Someone at the park said you got a roller coaster!"

"We didn't believe it," Lila put in.

"Well, it's true!" I announced. "Our friend Billy sent it. You know, the boy whose parents own Fantasy Forest?"

"We know," Lila said with a frown.

I smiled. Lila did not look happy. I knew why. Even *her* dad would never buy her a roller coaster. There was no way Lila could ever outdo the Wakester. That made me feel great.

11

Then I heard a car pull into the driveway.

"Mom's home," Steven said.

We all ran around to the front of the house. Mom had just parked our van in the garage.

"The roller coaster got here. The workmen are setting it up in the backyard," Elizabeth announced. "We love it!"

"Roller coaster?" Mom asked as she came out of the garage.

"Yes!" I squealed, throwing my arms around Mom's waist. "Thank you. Thank you so much!"

Mom smiled, but she looked confused. "What are you talking about? What roller coaster?" she asked.

My heart sank. "Billy sent it to us as a present," I said. "Didn't you know it was coming?"

"I'm as surprised as you are," Mom said, heading toward the backyard.

"Where are you going?" I called after her.

"To tell the workmen to stop putting the roller coaster together," Mom explained.

"Why?" Elizabeth wailed.

"Because we're not going to keep it," Mom explained.

"We'd better go," Eva said quietly to the others.

As our friends walked away, I pretended not to notice that Lila was the only one smiling now.

CHAPTER 3

What's There to Think About?

"There's Dad's car!" I announced. Mom had said we'd call Billy's parents when Dad got home. Elizabeth, Steven, and I were waiting for him near the living room window.

"Hi, kids," Dad said as he came in the door.

I ran to meet him. "Hi! Let me take your briefcase," I said.

"Are you thirsty?" Elizabeth asked. "I could get you something to drink."

"And, um, I could fetch your slippers," Steven offered.

Dad gave Steven a funny look. "I

don't even *own* a pair of slippers. What's going on? Why are you kids acting so wacky?"

"Well—," Elizabeth started.

I swallowed hard. What if Dad said we couldn't keep the roller coaster?

Mom came downstairs and gave Dad a kiss. "The kids got a present from Billy Grant today," she said.

"What is it?" Dad asked.

"A roller coaster," Steven said.

Dad burst out laughing. But he stopped when he saw how serious the rest of us looked. "A *real* roller coaster?" he asked.

I nodded. Elizabeth did too.

Dad looked stunned.

"We should call Billy's parents and find out what's going on," Mom explained.

"Good idea," Dad said.

We all piled into the den.

Dad found the Grants' number in

15

his book and dialed the phone. "Marc? Hi! This is Ned Wakefield. Listen, do you mind if I put you on the speaker phone? Alice and the kids are here too. Thanks." Dad pushed a button on the phone.

"Hello, Wakefields!" Billy's dad bellowed.

"Hi, Mr. Grant!" we all yelled.

"How do you like your roller coaster?" Mr. Grant asked.

"It's great!" I yelled as loudly as I could.

"Really super," Elizabeth added.

"Thanks for sending it," Steven said.

"I bet you had a bunch of kids waiting for it to arrive!" Mr. Grant said.

Elizabeth and I looked at each other.

"We didn't have *anyone* waiting," Steven spoke up. "We didn't know it was coming."

"You didn't know?" Mr. Grant sounded surprised. "Didn't you get our fax?"

"No," Dad reported.

"We sent it a couple of weeks back," Mr. Grant said. "We told you to call us if you didn't want the roller coaster. I guess that wasn't very good planning," he added with a chuckle.

Mr. Grant told us he had hired a man who lived in Sweet Valley to run the roller coaster for us. Then he started talking about insurance and stuff like that. I didn't understand any of it. But the longer Mr. Grant talked, the less worried Dad and Mom seemed.

"Billy really wanted you guys to have the roller coaster," Mr. Grant explained. "But of course we'll take it back if you don't want it."

"We want it!" I yelled.

"I think we'd better give you a call later," Dad told Mr. Grant. "We need to have a family meeting before we decide."

"No problem!" Mr. Grant said.

I smiled at Elizabeth. At least Mom and Dad hadn't said no—yet.

Dad hung up the phone. "Listen, kids," he said in his let's-be-reasonable voice. "Our backyard is no place for a roller coaster."

"The roller coaster isn't that big," Steven argued. "I'm sure it won't be much trouble."

"We'll take care of it ourselves," Elizabeth added. "You won't have to do a thing."

"Sorry, kids. But I agree with your dad," Mom said, and shook her head. "Roller coasters are fun. But we don't need one in our backyard."

"Please let us keep it for a little while," I begged.

But Dad shook his head firmly. "Sorry, but the roller coaster has to go. I'll call Mr. Grant after dinner and tell him."

If Mom and Dad give back the roller coaster, everyone at school will laugh, I thought. *And everyone will start talking about Lila's pool party again.* A fat tear rolled down my cheek.

Elizabeth's bottom lip was quivering. Even Steven had tears in his eyes.

Mom hates to see us cry. "Come on, kids," she said. "Don't take it so hard."

"I—I can't help it," I sobbed.

"Me neither," Elizabeth said.

Steven sniffled hard.

Mom looked at Dad. "Well, maybe we don't have to call Mr. Grant tonight. We could sleep on our decision."

"Hurray!" Elizabeth and I shouted.

"Thanks, Mom and Dad," Steven said. "I'm sure you won't regret this."

"We're just going to *think* about it," Dad reminded all of us.

Elizabeth and I looked at each other happily. As long as Mom and Dad hadn't made up their minds yet, we could *help* them make the right decision. And I already had an idea of how to do that.

CHAPTER 4

Breakfast in Bed

Before we left for school the next morning, Elizabeth and I knocked on the door of our parents' bedroom.

"Come in!" Mom called in a sleepy voice.

I opened the door. Elizabeth walked into Mom and Dad's room with a tray of food.

"What's this?" Dad asked as he sat up in bed.

"A surprise!" I said. "Breakfast in bed!"

Mom sat up and examined the tray. "Did you girls do all of this yourselves?"

she asked in a delighted voice.

"Steven helped," Elizabeth said.

"We would never, ever use the stove without his help," I said in a goody-goody voice. "We're too responsible for that."

Elizabeth rolled her eyes at me.

Dad looked amused. "This looks wonderful!" he said.

I think Dad was just being nice. The truth was the food looked a little *weird*. The scrambled eggs were a light green color, and a few pieces of eggshell were sticking out. The coffee Steven had made was *lumpy*. But at least the toast looked OK—it was only a little burned.

"Have some eggs." Mom handed Dad a fork.

"After you," Dad said, making a face.

Just then the doorbell rang.

"I'll get it!" Mom quickly moved the tray onto Dad's lap.

Dad put the tray on the bedside table. "I'll help!" he offered.

Mom and Dad both dashed out of the bedroom. Elizabeth and I looked at each other. Mom and Dad were sure acting weird! It was almost as if they didn't want their breakfast in bed.

Elizabeth and I followed our parents to the front door. Steven came out from the kitchen and joined us.

Mom opened the door. A workman from Fantasy Forest was standing there.

"Good morning, folks," the workman said. "We were wondering if we could get back to work now."

"Well—," Dad started.

"I don't know . . . ," Mom said.

"Please," Elizabeth and I begged.

"We'll do all the work taking care of it. You won't even know it's there," Steven said.

"Oh, OK," Dad said.

Mom looked at Dad like she thought he was crazy. But then she shrugged. "Fine," she agreed.

Our breakfast in bed really must have worked!

"Can we stay home from school and watch the workmen?" I asked.

"Don't push your luck," Mom told me.

When we got home from school that afternoon, the Wakester was all put together in our backyard! It wasn't the *biggest* roller coaster I'd ever seen. But it was the most *beautiful*. It had cute red and purple cars, and a big metal hill that was taller than our whole house!

"Wow!" Ellen said from behind me. Almost all of our friends from Mrs. Otis's class had come home with us. A bunch of Steven's friends were there too. Lila hadn't wanted to come.

A man in a bright red suit with gold buttons was sitting in one of our yard chairs, reading a magazine. When he saw us, he got up and came toward us with a smile.

"Hello," the man said cheerfully. "My name is George. The Grants hired me to run your roller coaster for you."

George gestured toward the roller coaster as if we were princesses and princes entering a royal palace. "Would anyone like a ride?" he asked.

"I would!" I shouted.

"Me too!" Elizabeth yelled.

All of our friends started yelling for rides too.

"Step this way," George said.

Elizabeth and I got into the first car. Ellen and Eva were in the second one, Amy and Todd were in the third, and two of Steven's friends were behind them. Since the Wakester had only four cars, the rest of our friends had to wait.

George pushed a button. The Wakester started to move.

I grabbed Elizabeth's hand as our little car reached the top of the big hill. We stopped there for a moment and then rushed down the other side.

Elizabeth and I screamed. It was just as scary as a big roller coaster in an amusement park!

"Ya-hoo!" Steven hooted.

We went up and down a few hills and around a big turn. Then we rolled back to where we had started.

"That was fun!" Elizabeth exclaimed.

"Can we go again?" I asked George.

"Of course," George said. "This is your roller coaster. You can ride it as much as you like."

Amy and Todd got out to let Winston and Lois have a turn. Elizabeth and I didn't move from our car.

"I don't want to get off until dinnertime," I told Elizabeth.

Elizabeth grinned broadly. "Or maybe *bedtime!* I'm having so much fun."

"Me too," I agreed. "Getting the Wakester is the best thing that's ever happened to us!"

CHAPTER 5
Invitations

"Are you the Wakefield twins?" a girl with blond braids asked Elizabeth and me at school the next morning.

Elizabeth nodded.

"I heard about your roller coaster!" the girl said. "You guys are so lucky! I *love* roller coasters."

"Would you like to ride ours?" I asked.

"Sure!" the girl exclaimed.

"Come by any time," I said. "And bring your friends."

"Thanks, I will!" the girl said.

"Do you know her?" Elizabeth asked after the girl had gone up the stairs.

"Nope," I said. "I think she's in the third grade."

"She had braces," Elizabeth pointed out. "I bet she's in the fourth grade *at least.*"

"Cool," I said. The older kids at our school hardly ever talked to second-graders. But big kids had been coming up to us all morning. On the bus, a boy I didn't even know had even given me the potato chips out of his lunch! Our roller coaster was making us really popular!

Elizabeth and I walked into Mrs. Otis's room. All of our friends ran up to us.

"We had so much fun yesterday," Eva said.

"I screamed so much, my throat is sore," Ellen added.

"I asked Mrs. Otis if you could talk

about the Wakester during show-and-tell," Caroline Pearce told us. "Since I didn't get a turn yesterday, I want to hear all about it!"

I smiled at Caroline. "Thanks! I'll make sure you get a ride this afternoon."

"OK," Caroline said with a grin.

Lila came up to our group. She was holding a stack of pink envelopes. "Eva, this is for you," Lila said proudly. "Ellen, this is yours."

I knew what was in those envelopes: invitations to Lila's party.

Caroline looked down at the ground. She probably felt funny because she wouldn't get one. Lila hardly ever talks to Caroline. Or Lois. Or Suzie. Lila is very choosy about her friends. Actually, she's kind of a snob.

"Here, Caroline," Lila said sweetly, handing her an invitation.

Caroline's eyes almost popped out of her head. "Thanks," she said happily.

"Is Lois here?" Lila asked.

"Right here!" Lois said.

"I hope you can come!" Lila handed Lois a pink envelope.

"You *do?* I mean, thanks!" Lois said.

"How many kids are you inviting?" I asked Lila.

"All the girls in our class," Lila replied.

Elizabeth smiled at Lila as she took her invitation. She probably thought Lila was just being nice.

I knew better. What Lila was trying to do was take attention away from the Wakester. What a fink!

"Here, Jessica." Lila smiled as she handed me my invitation.

I did not smile back.

Eva ripped open her invitation.

"This is so pretty," she said, touching the lacy white card.

"Thanks," Lila said.

"I can't wait for the party," Elizabeth told Lila.

"Well, I can't wait for this afternoon," I said loudly. "Who's coming over to my house after school to ride my roller coaster?"

"I am!" Amy said.

"Me too," Suzie added.

Lila gave me an angry look. "Aren't you going to open your invitation to my party?"

"Maybe later," I said in my best I-don't-care voice. "Elizabeth and I have to plan what to say during show-and-tell. Mrs. Otis said we could talk about the Wakester."

"But I wanted to talk about my party!" Lila wailed.

I stuck my tongue out at Lila. "Too bad!" I said.

"We can leave time for Lila," Elizabeth said.

"No way!" I yelled. "We need *all* of the time, Lizzie. The Wakester is the biggest thing that has ever happened to Sweet Valley. It's much more important than Lila's stupid party!"

Lila's mouth dropped open. "My party is *not* stupid. You take that back!"

"Stupid, stupid, stupid!" I chanted right in Lila's face.

Lila's eyes blazed with anger. She reached out and snatched my invitation out of my hand. "Guess what? You're not invited to my party anymore."

My throat tightened up. I didn't think Lila would do something like that! I felt like running away. But everyone was watching me. So I put my hands on my hips and gave Lila a nasty look. "I don't need your dumb old party!" I told her. "I can just stay home and ride my roller coaster. That will be twice as much fun!"

Lila's face was bright red. "Jessica Wakefield, you are not my friend anymore!" she screamed. Then she turned and stomped away.

Who cares? I thought. *Everyone in the whole school wants to be my friend. Who needs Lila?*

CHAPTER 6

A Crowd

"Where's everyone going?" the bus driver asked that afternoon. Everyone was getting off the bus at our stop.

"To my house," I said proudly. "We have a roller coaster in our backyard."

"Wow!" the bus driver said. He looked impressed.

Steven hopped off the bus first. "Follow me!" he said, leading the way down our street.

"You can go on the first ride with me," I told Caroline as we followed the other kids toward our house.

But when we got to our backyard, the Wakester was already running! Dozens of kids were waiting in line to get on.

"How did they all get here so fast?" Elizabeth asked. "School just let out."

"I think some of these kids are from the middle school," Steven told her. "They get out earlier than we do."

"Middle schoolers?" I said. *I'm going to be the most popular second-grader in the history of the world!* I added to myself.

"Do we have to wait in line?" Caroline whined. "You said I could go on it right away!"

Ellen put her hands on her hips. "I don't want to wait either," she said.

"Your best friends shouldn't have to wait while *strangers* ride your roller coaster," Caroline said to me.

Caroline wasn't my best friend. But I kind of knew what she meant. I looked at Elizabeth.

Elizabeth shrugged.

"Well, I guess we could go to the front," I said.

"Great!" Caroline said. She grabbed Ellen's hand, and they marched to the front of the line. I followed them.

"Hey, what are Ellen and Caroline doing?" Todd called out.

"They're cutting in line!" Steven's friend Joe yelled.

Winston marched over to Ellen and Caroline. "You guys have to wait your turn!" he said.

"Jessica said it was OK," Ellen argued.

The Wakester stopped, and a bunch of kids got off. Caroline started to get in the front car. But Winston grabbed her arm and stopped her.

"It's not your turn!" Winston yelled.

"Mind your own business!" Caroline said, and gave Winston a shove. He fell down on the ground.

"That's enough!" George said. "I'm not starting the ride again until you girls go to the back of the line."

Caroline put her hands on her hips. "Jessica, do something!"

"Sorry, Caroline," I said. "But George is in charge."

Caroline and Ellen looked mad. But they still stomped to the back of the line. Then George started up the ride again.

Elizabeth turned to me. "Do you want to get in line?" she asked.

I shook my head. "Let's go get our snack," I said.

Elizabeth and I went into the house. We found two older boys—they looked like sixth-graders—in our kitchen.

"Who are you?" Elizabeth demanded.

I looked at the kitchen table. When Mom is busy with work, she always leaves our snack out for us. But there was nothing on the table except for two *empty* plates.

"What happened to our snack?" I demanded.

"We ate it!" one of the boys said. He had crumbs around his mouth.

The other boy laughed. "Yeah. It wasn't bad, for granola!" He and his friend ran out the door, laughing.

"I don't believe this!" Elizabeth said.

I sighed. "Let's ask Mom what else there is to eat."

Elizabeth made a face. "We'd better not."

"Why not?" I asked.

"Because we told Mom we could take care of the Wakester ourselves,"

Elizabeth reminded me. "What will she think if we tell her some boys came into the house and stole our snack?"

My stomach was growling, but I wanted to be brave. "I guess I can live without it," I said.

Elizabeth and I went back outside and got in line. We had to wait half an hour before we could get onto our own roller coaster! Even then, the ride didn't seem half as much fun as it had the day before.

"Kids, come outside, please!" Mom called just before dinnertime. Everyone had gone home, even George.

Elizabeth and I ran outside.

"Look at this mess!" Mom said, pointing at the backyard. It was a disaster. Candy wrappers, stray pieces of notebook paper, empty soda cans, and even a spelling book were spread across the grass.

"Get some garbage bags," Mom told Elizabeth and me. "You kids need to clean this up before we eat."

I did not want to clean up the backyard. I hate cleaning, even when it's my own mess. And this wasn't.

"But I was watching cartoons on TV," I said.

"And I was doing my homework," Elizabeth added.

Mom shrugged. "Those things will have to wait. I want this mess cleaned up, pronto. I'll get Steven to come down and help." She went inside.

"I'll get the garbage bags," Elizabeth said with a frown.

I didn't answer. I wanted to scream and stomp my feet. But I couldn't. Responsible kids who deserve roller coasters don't do those kinds of things.

Elizabeth came outside with the bags. She handed me one.

Steven stormed outside. "This stinks!" he grumbled as he picked up a banana peel.

"Doing a little extra work isn't a big deal," Elizabeth said. "The Wakester is worth it."

I wasn't so sure. So far, the Wakester had made me have a big fight with Lila and get *uninvited* to her party. I spent all afternoon breaking up fights between my friends and waiting in line. And I didn't even get a snack! Having the Wakester wasn't half as much fun as I thought it would be.

But Elizabeth and Steven loved the roller coaster. I didn't want to ruin it for them. So I pretended to love it too.

CHAPTER 7
A Bigger Crowd

"I'm going up to our room," Elizabeth told me after school the next day.

"Why?" I demanded. "Most of our friends are here." The crowd of kids in our yard was even bigger than it had been the day before.

"I know," Elizabeth said. "But, um, my stomach hurts a little. I think I'll just read."

"OK," I said. I felt a little lonely as I watched Elizabeth walk into the house. School that day had been a bummer. Lila wouldn't even talk to me. And everyone who did talk to me only wanted to talk about the Wakester. Now my own twin sister wouldn't play with me!

I walked over to Eva and Amy. "Hi, you guys! Do you want to jump rope with me?" I asked.

"No, we're almost to the front of the line," Eva said.

"I can wait until after you get off the Wakester," I offered.

"But I want to see how many times I can ride it before dinner," Amy said.

"Me too!" Eva said.

"But I don't feel like riding the Wakester," I whined.

"You could jump rope by yourself," Eva suggested.

No thanks! I thought, and stomped away. My friends were at my house every afternoon. But I was beginning to think it wasn't because they liked me. They were only interested in riding our roller coaster.

Steven walked toward me, carrying his basketball. "Hey, Jess! Want to shoot some hoops?"

I gave Steven a funny look. Steven never, ever lets me play basketball with him. He says I'm too short.

"Why aren't you playing with your friends?" I asked.

"I asked them," Steven admitted. "But they want to ride the roller coaster."

"Well . . . ," I started. Steven had said no to me so many times, I felt like saying no to him. And I didn't want Steven to think I would play with him whenever *he* wanted.

"Never mind!" Steven said angrily, and walked away.

I walked the other way—back toward the line.

"Jessica, over here!" Ellen called.

She was standing in line with Julie Porter.

I was happy to see Ellen and Julie. I ran over to them.

"Come ride with us!" Julie called.

I gave up. "OK."

Julie stepped back to make room for me, and I stepped into the line.

"What do you think you're doing?" someone behind me demanded. I turned around. It was a boy I'd never seen before.

"I'm getting in line," I told him.

"Cutting is against the rules," the boy said. "You'd better go to the end of the line before I tell one of the Wakefields."

"But I . . ." I couldn't finish my sentence. I was so mad, I couldn't speak.

The boy started to laugh.

I stomped my foot and wished Lila was around. *She* was great at telling people off.

"Forget it," I told Ellen and Julie. Then I stomped off toward the park.

I had to find a way to get rid of the roller coaster. But since Elizabeth and Steven loved it, I would have to do it *secretly*. The only question was, how?

CHAPTER 8

An Idea

"So, are you kids liking the roller coaster?" Dad asked the next morning at breakfast.

Steven, Elizabeth, and I looked at each other.

"Um, it's great," I said.

"Yeah, really . . . great," Elizabeth said brightly.

Steven nodded. "Great."

Mom smiled as Dad filled up her cup of coffee. "You wouldn't believe how many kids were here yesterday afternoon," she told him. "We're going to put the park out of business."

"Any problem with the neighbors?" Dad asked as he sat back down.

"Nope," Mom said. "They've been very understanding. Especially considering how noisy it got yesterday afternoon."

I wish the neighbors would *complain,* I thought. *Maybe I could talk them into it.* Then I had a perfect idea!

"May I be excused?" I asked quickly.

"Sure," Mom said. "Are you OK?"

"Fine!" I said as I hurried out of the kitchen. I was better than fine. I was terrific! I had figured out how to get rid of the Wakester!

I don't need to wait for the neighbors to complain! I thought as I locked myself into the room I shared with my sister. *I could pretend to be a neighbor and complain myself!*

My desk was a mess. I couldn't find my own paper. So I got a piece of

Elizabeth's special green paper out of her desk. Then I sat down at my desk.

"Dear Mom and Dad," I wrote. *Oops!* I thought with a giggle. The neighbors wouldn't call Mom and Dad *that!*

I crumpled up that piece of paper and got a new one.

"Dear Ned and Alice," I wrote. *What else should I say?* I wondered. I wanted to use big words so Mom and Dad would really believe a grown-up had written the letter.

I was chewing on my pen when Elizabeth banged on the door. "We've got to go soon!" she yelled.

"OK! I'll be there in a minute!" I called. I finished the letter as quickly as possible.

This is what it said:

"Dear Ned and Alice,
    The Wakester has to go! It is noisy. There are too many kids

in your yard after school. Some of them steal things like food. And they shouldn't throw trash on the ground like that.

Signed, a naybore"

I didn't have time to read the letter over. But I wasn't worried. I'm not as good a speller as my sister, but I'm not bad either. I was sure the letter was fine.

I quickly searched through Elizabeth's desk until I found an envelope. I folded up the letter and stuck it inside. Then I sealed it and wrote our address on the front.

"The bus is coming!" Elizabeth screamed. "I see it!"

I found a stamp, licked it, and stuck it on the envelope.

"Let's go!" I yelled, throwing open the door.

Elizabeth and I ran down the

stairs, out the door, and down the street. We caught the bus just before it pulled away from the curb.

"Whew!" Elizabeth said as we fell into a bus seat. "That was close."

"I know!" I said. I was trying to think up a really good reason why I had locked myself in our room. Elizabeth would definitely want to know why. After all, I had almost made us miss the bus.

I could tell Elizabeth I was wrapping her birthday present. But our birthday wasn't for months. I could say I was talking to Lila on the phone about something secret. Only Lila wasn't talking to me anymore.

I looked at Elizabeth. She was studying for a spelling test. The bus got all the way to school, and Elizabeth still hadn't asked me anything.

We got off the bus. Elizabeth ran to

play tag with Amy and Todd. I stopped at the mailbox in front of our school and mailed my letter. I felt pretty smart. Maybe fooling Elizabeth wasn't that hard after all.

CHAPTER 9

Mrs. Zwibbons

The next day after school, Elizabeth and I went inside to get our snack—before anyone else did. Our backyard was just as crowded as ever. "Did you get the mail yet?" I asked Mom.

"Sure did," Mom said. "Nothing but bills and magazines."

I frowned. "Are you *sure?*"

"Positive," Mom said.

"Darn," I mumbled.

"What?" Mom asked.

"Er, delightful," I said. "Those peanut butter sandwiches really look great."

Mom gave me a funny look. "Thanks," she said.

The phone rang.

"I'll get it!" I ran to the phone and picked it up. "Wakefield residence," I said in my most polite voice.

"Hello there, dearie," came an odd, squeaky voice. "Can I speak to your mother, please?"

For a second I thought one of my friends was crank calling me. But then I remembered that everyone I knew was in my backyard.

"May I tell her who's calling?" I asked.

"Mrs. Zwibbons," the strange voice said.

"OK. Just a minute," I said. I held the phone out to Mom. "It's Mrs. Zwibbons on the phone for you."

Mom handed a sandwich to Elizabeth. She gave another to me. She put Steven's sandwich in the refrigerator for when he came home from basketball practice. Then Mom took the phone.

"Hello?" Mom asked. Then she frowned.

Elizabeth and I listened while we chewed.

"I'm very sorry it's been bothering you," Mom said into the phone. "Well, that's true. Kids *can* make a lot of noise."

Elizabeth raised her eyebrows. Was Mrs. Zwibbons complaining about the Wakester?

Yahoo! I thought. I took a big bite of my sandwich so Elizabeth wouldn't see that I was smiling.

"Well, you are the only person to complain," Mom continued. "I don't think we should ask the kids to give up the roller coaster. But I *will* ask them to keep the noise down. Please call back if the noise is still bothering you. OK, Mrs. Zwibbons, good-bye now." Mom hung up the phone.

"Is someone upset about the roller coaster?" Elizabeth asked.

"Yes," Mom said. "You kids will have to ask your friends to be a little quieter."

"We will," I said. *Not!* I added to myself.

Mom was still looking thoughtfully at the phone. "Do you kids know a Mrs. Zwibbons who lives around here?"

"No," I said.

Elizabeth had her mouth full. She shook her head.

"I wonder who she could be?" Mom wondered. "She seemed to know us."

I didn't know who Mrs. Zwibbons was. And I didn't care either. I just hoped she was very good at complaining.

CHAPTER 10
Mail Call!

"Come on, Jess," Elizabeth said on Saturday morning. "Let's ride the roller coaster."

"The line's too long," I whined. I felt grumpy, grouchy, and gruff. My backyard was full of kids. But none of them were my friends. All of my *real* friends were going to Lila's party.

Except for Elizabeth. Elizabeth had stayed home from Lila's party to keep me company. I knew Elizabeth was trying to cheer me up, but I just didn't feel cheery.

The letter I had sent to Mom and

Dad hadn't arrived yet. I thought it must have gotten lost in the mail. So I'd sent another letter yesterday. But I wished I could think of something else to do to get rid of the Wakester.

"Please ride the Wakester with me," Elizabeth begged.

"Well . . . OK," I agreed.

"I have to tell you something about the roller coaster," Elizabeth said once we were in line.

"OK," I said.

Elizabeth took a deep breath. "Don't get mad," she started. "But, well, um, see—"

"Jessica! Elizabeth! Steven!" Mom called us from the back door. "Come inside for a minute. I want to talk to you!"

Elizabeth and I ran inside together. Steven had been climbing a tree. He jumped down and ran after us.

Mom was waiting for us in the

kitchen. She was holding one of the letters I had written!

"Kids, I want to read something to you," Mom said.

My hands got sweaty when I thought about how fast I had written that letter. Would it fool everybody? As Mom started to read, I watched their faces.

Elizabeth and Steven were looking down at the table. I couldn't see their faces very well, so I couldn't be sure if I'd fooled them.

"It's signed 'A Neighbor,'" Mom finished. She set the letter down. She looked like she thought something was funny. Did she think my letter was funny?

"Do we get to—I mean, do we *have* to get rid of the Wakester?" Steven asked.

Say yes! I begged Mom silently.

"What do you kids think we should do?" Mom asked.

Steven shrugged.

"I don't know," Elizabeth said.

"I don't want you to get in trouble," I told Mom.

"Don't worry about that," Mom said with a smile. "What I want to know is, do you kids still like the roller coaster?"

I wanted to tell Mom how I really felt. But I just couldn't. If I did, Elizabeth and Steven would be really mad at me.

"I think the roller coaster is totally neat," I said.

Elizabeth nodded slowly. "*I* don't want to get rid of it."

"Me neither," Steven added.

"Well . . . OK," Mom said. "But if you really want to keep it, you and your friends will have to be quieter."

I couldn't believe it. Mom was going to let us keep the Wakester—even after two people had complained! And one of them, Mrs. Zwibbons, wasn't even me!

"Do you want to talk to us about anything else?" Elizabeth asked.

Mom shook her head. She carefully folded up my letter. "That's it. You kids can go outside and enjoy the roller coaster now."

Enjoy the roller coaster? I thought as I followed Elizabeth outside. *Ha! That was funny.*

Elizabeth didn't say anything as we got back in line. I was disappointed. My plan had failed. Unless I could think of a new one, I'd be stuck with the Wakester forever!

CHAPTER 11
Party Problems

"There are Eva and Ellen!" Elizabeth exclaimed later that day. We had just gotten off the Wakester.

"They're supposed to be at Lila's party," I said. "What are they doing here?"

"I don't know," Elizabeth said. "Let's go ask them!"

Elizabeth and I ran over to our friends.

"Why aren't you at Lila's?" Elizabeth asked.

"The party was called off," Eva explained.

My jaw dropped. "Why?"

"The pump in Lila's pool is broken," Ellen said. "That makes the pool unsafe to swim in."

"Poor Lila," Elizabeth said.

"She sounded really upset when she called to tell me the party was canceled," Eva said.

Ellen nodded sadly. "I asked Lila to come over here with us. But she won't because—" Ellen looked at me. "Well, you know."

I should have felt happy. Our friends wouldn't be having fun at Lila's party. They wouldn't be talking about it at school on Monday. And Lila wouldn't get to be the center of attention.

But I didn't feel happy. I felt sorry for Lila. And I was sick of fighting with her. But I didn't know how to make her *unmad* at me.

Elizabeth looked at the roller coaster.

"Do you think Lila would want to have her party here?" she asked. "She could still be the host. We would just sort of lend her the Wakester for free."

I smiled. My sister could be pretty smart sometimes.

"I don't know," Ellen said.

"We could ask Lila," I suggested.

"We should get permission first," Elizabeth said.

"You ask Mom," I told her. "I'll call Lila."

Elizabeth and I ran toward the house. Eva and Ellen were right behind us.

"You're never going to talk Lila into this," Ellen said as we piled into the house.

"Just you wait!" I told her.

"Do you want to ride the Wakester?" I asked Lila about an hour and a half later.

I had called Lila and told her about Elizabeth's idea. At first, Lila thought I was trying to trick her. I promised I wasn't. Finally, Lila admitted she still wanted to have the party. She called all of her guests and told them the party was back on—at my house! It felt a little funny to be nice to Lila after being angry at her for so long. But I was a lot happier now.

"Sure, I'll try it," Lila said.

"Great!" I said. "Sit with me in the very front. That's the best seat."

"OK," Lila agreed.

I couldn't resist bragging a little. "Lots of people were here earlier," I told Lila as we climbed onto the ride. "But Mom, Dad, Elizabeth, and I kicked them all out. We told them the Wakester was reserved for a 'Private Party' this afternoon."

"*My* party," Lila said firmly.

"Right," I agreed.

"Hang on!" George cried as he started up the Wakester. At first Lila pretended she wasn't having a good time. But as we started down the first big drop, she let out a great big scream. When the ride was over, she was smiling.

"Wasn't that fun?" I asked.

"Yeah. Having your own roller coaster must be pretty cool," Lila admitted. Then her face turned red. "I—I'm sorry I wouldn't come over and ride it sooner. I guess I was jealous."

"I understand," I said. "And I'm sorry I pretended that your party wasn't a big deal. I guess I was jealous too."

Lila smiled at me.

I felt great. I had my best friend back again!

"Do you want another ride?" Lila asked me.

"If you do," I said with a shrug.

Lila's eyes widened. "You *don't?*"

I leaned closer to Lila. "You know what? I'm totally sick of the Wakester," I whispered. *Wow! It felt good to say that,* I thought.

Lila stared at me for a minute. "Why are you sick of the roller coaster?" she asked me as we climbed out of our seats.

"Shh!" I said. "I don't want Elizabeth to know. She *loves* the Wakester. But I'm sick of having kids in my backyard all the time. And I'm tired of everyone acting like they're my friends, leaving garbage that *I* have to clean up, and eating my snacks!"

"So why don't you get rid of it?" Lila asked.

"I tried!" I told her. "But my plan didn't work." I told Lila about the letters I had written.

Lila put an arm around my shoulder. "Don't worry. I'll help you get rid of it."

"How?" I asked.

"I don't know yet," Lila admitted. "But I'll think of something."

Maybe Lila wasn't just being nice. She probably wanted to help get rid of the roller coaster so she could be the center of attention again. But I didn't care. I'd learned that being popular wasn't that great. But I didn't tell Lila that. She never would have believed me.

CHAPTER 12
Lila's Plan

"What's that noise?" Ellen asked in a sleepy voice early the next morning.

"It sounds like a radio," Julie said.

"With huge speakers," Eva put in.

"Right under the window!" Lila grumbled.

"Be quiet, you guys!" I crawled further down into my sleeping bag and pulled the top over my head.

Mom and Dad had let a bunch of our friends sleep over last night. We had stayed up really late telling ghost stories.

Just the *thought* of waking up early made me crabby. But I still couldn't go back to sleep. The noise was much too loud. I crawled out of my sleeping bag and went to the window to see what was going on.

"Someone is setting up a picnic in our backyard!" I reported. "They have a blanket, a basket of food, and a really big radio."

Elizabeth jumped out of her bed and came to see. "Do they think our yard is a park or something?"

I recognized one of the kids sitting on the blanket outside our window. "It's Charlie Cashman!" I exclaimed.

"Ew!" about six of our friends said all at once. None of the girls in my class could stand Charlie. He's a big bully. He even steals milk money from first-graders.

I backed away from the window in horror. "I can't believe Charlie is having a picnic in my backyard!"

Lila sat up in her sleeping bag. "If you ask me, having the Wakester sounds like a big pain."

I looked at Lila. I hoped she wouldn't tell Elizabeth my secret.

"I like riding the Wakester," Lois said. "But I'm glad it's not in *my* yard."

Elizabeth sat down on her bed and sighed. "Actually, I am kind of sick of it," she whispered.

I was too surprised to say anything. I just stared at my sister.

Elizabeth looked back at me. "I'm sorry, Jessica! I know how much you love the Wakester, but it's driving me crazy!"

I started to giggle, and then to laugh.

Elizabeth looked puzzled. "What's so funny?" she asked.

"I'm sick of the Wakester too," I

admitted. "I wanted to get rid of it. But *I* thought *you* liked it."

Elizabeth's eyes lit up. "Oh, Jess, that's great!" she said, laughing.

"I don't understand," Ellen said. "I think the roller coaster is totally cool. Ever since you got it, everyone wants to play at your house."

"But they don't want to play with *us*," Elizabeth said.

"They just want to ride the Wakester," I added.

"That's not true!" Amy said. "We'd still like you even if you didn't have the Wakester."

"Really?" Elizabeth asked.

"Yup!" Eva said.

"But if we ask Mom and Dad to get rid of the Wakester, Steven will be furious," Elizabeth said.

"You're right," I said.

Elizabeth bit her lip. "I guess we're stuck with it."

"No you're not!" Lila said. "You just have to be sneaky about how you get rid of it."

I'm good at being sneaky, but Lila is a hundred times better. "Do you have a plan?" I asked her.

Lila gave me a big smile. "Of course I have a plan. But I'm going to need everyone's help. . . ."

CHAPTER 13

Annoying Neighbors

*B*rrring! The phone in the kitchen rang loudly.

Mom covered her eyes with her hands. "Ned, would you please get that?" she asked. "I have a headache."

Brrring!

Dad groaned. "Let the machine get it. I'm trying to eat my dinner."

Brrring!

I looked down at my plate. I knew if I looked at Elizabeth, I would start to laugh.

The answering machine clicked on.

Our phone had been ringing every

five minutes for hours. It had started just after our friends had left to go home that afternoon.

"How many calls have we gotten so far?" Steven asked. He'd been over at Joe's all afternoon.

Mom did a silent count. "About five dozen."

Steven let out a low whistle. "Sixty calls! The neighbors must be really mad at us."

"They say that the roller coaster is too noisy," Mom said.

"And that people are parking their cars in front of their driveways," Dad added.

"And that kids cut through their yards to get here," Mom said.

Elizabeth looked at me and shook her head. I knew what she was thinking. Our friends sure were good at complaining!

The calls were Lila's idea. Every

five minutes one of the girls who had stayed over would call our house, disguise her voice, and pretend to be a neighbor. Poor Dad and Mom! The calls were driving them nuts. But that meant Lila's plan was working.

Brrring! The phone rang again.

Dad pushed his plate away. "I'll get that," he said.

"But what about your dinner?" Mom asked.

"I can't eat with the phone ringing constantly," Dad said and picked up the phone.

"Hello, Wakefield residence," Dad said angrily. "Oh, the roller coaster is bothering you, eh? Well, guess what? It won't be bothering you much longer. We're getting rid of it! That's right!" Dad banged down the phone without saying good-bye.

Steven's eyes were wide. "Why did you say that?"

Dad slumped down in his seat. He didn't look angry anymore. "I'm sorry, kids," he said quietly. "But I can't deal with the, uh, *neighbors* anymore. We have to get rid of the roller coaster."

"Really?" Steven said. "Gee, that's too bad. But I guess I understand."

Elizabeth got up and patted Dad on the back. "Don't worry, Dad. We're not mad."

I did my best to look sad. "What will we do with the roller coaster?" I asked.

"I don't know," Mom said. "But I'll make some calls in the morning. Maybe one of the local parks will take it off our hands."

"That's a good idea!" Elizabeth said. "That way the neighbors would be happy, and we could still ride the Wakester whenever we wanted."

Brrring!

We all groaned together.

"Let the answering machine get it," Dad suggested.

"May we be excused?" I asked.

"Sure," Mom said.

Elizabeth and I ran up the stairs to our room.

"Do you think they know that it was our friends who were calling?" Elizabeth asked me.

"Not a chance!" I said.

"Steven can't blame us now," Elizabeth said with a giggle.

"I know," I said happily. "We're the sneakiest twin sisters in Sweet Valley!"

CHAPTER 14

Mrs. Zwibbons— Uncovered!

"Most of the ride is down," Elizabeth said the next afternoon. We were sitting in our backyard, watching the workmen take down the roller coaster.

"It looks sort of sad," I said.

"They're going to start putting the roller coaster back together at Secca Lake right away," Mom said. "We can go ride it next weekend."

I didn't really want to go ride the Wakester. But I didn't want Mom to know how I really felt. "That would be great," I said.

Dad joined us. He threw the day's mail in Mom's lap.

Mom sorted through it. "Oh, no. More hate mail from the neighbors," Mom said. She opened one of the letters and read it. "You know, it's funny," Mom said. "This neighbor says she's a librarian."

"I don't think that's strange at all," Elizabeth said quickly. "Librarians like things quiet."

"True," Mom admitted. "But what's strange is that she misspelled 'neighbor.' Librarians are usually good spellers. Do you know how to spell 'neighbor,' Elizabeth?"

"Sure!" Elizabeth said, glancing nervously at me.

"Let's hear it," Mom said.

"N-i-e-g-h-b-o-r," Elizabeth said slowly.

Mom shook her head no. "Isn't that funny! That's just how this 'librarian' spelled it too."

Elizabeth's face was bright red. "I wrote that letter," she admitted. "I wanted us to get rid of the Wakester. It was getting on my nerves."

"Wow," Steven said.

"You should have just told us the truth," Dad told Elizabeth.

"I know," Elizabeth said. "I'm sorry."

"So who can tell us how to spell 'neighbor'?" Mom asked after she'd opened another letter.

"I can!" I said in my champion-speller voice. "You spell it just the way it sounds: n-a-y-b-o-r-e."

Steven looked at me like I was crazy.

"Not even close," Dad said with a grin.

Mom tossed the other letter I'd sent into my lap. "So, I guess this letter is from you."

"Yes, it is," I confessed sadly. Then I turned to Steven. "I'm sorry,

Steven. But I wanted to get rid of the roller coaster too."

Steven shook his head in amazement. "Were those *your* friends who were calling?"

I glanced at Mom and Dad. "Um, well, yeah," I said.

"We knew," Mom said.

"Really?" I asked.

Dad nodded.

"Are you mad at us?" I asked Steven.

"Not really," he said in a squeaky voice. "I wanted to get rid of the roller coaster too."

My jaw dropped. "You're Mrs. Zwibbons!" I said to Steven.

"No way!" Elizabeth exclaimed.

"Pleased to make your acquaintance," Steven said in his Mrs. Zwibbons voice.

Mom laughed. "I knew I recognized that voice from somewhere!"

"So you all wanted to get rid of the

88

Wakester," Dad said. "Are you happy now?"

"Well, things do seem awfully quiet around here," Steven said.

"Yeah. I have the solution to that. We should get a pet!" Elizabeth said. "We could take care of it ourselves."

"How about a bunny?" I suggested.

"Or a snake!" Steven said.

"No way!" Dad replied.

"Absolutely not," Mom agreed. "We've had enough excitement around here for now."

"I like the quiet," Dad said.

Steven, Elizabeth, and I smiled at each other. I knew what we were thinking: The quiet was all right, at least for today.

"So now that we have some time to ourselves," Mom announced, "we need to talk about what you girls want to wear in your school pictures.

Class picture day is coming up, you know."

"Well, we *have* to match," I said. "I want us to wear our new yellow dresses. We'll be the prettiest girls in class."

"I don't want to get too dressed up for school," Elizabeth argued. "I don't want anything to happen to our nice new clothes. What if we have to paint in class or something?"

"Come on, Lizzie. We have to look our best. What could possibly go wrong?" I asked.

This year's class picture could be the messiest one ever! Find out why in Sweet Valley Kids #69, **CLASS PICTURE DAY!**

SIGN UP FOR THE SWEET VALLEY HIGH® FAN CLUB!

Hey, girls! Get all the gossip on Sweet Valley High's® most popular teenagers when you join our fantastic Fan Club! As a member, you'll get all of this really cool stuff:

- Membership Card with your own personal Fan Club ID number
- A Sweet Valley High® Secret Treasure Box
- Sweet Valley High® Stationery
- Official Fan Club Pencil (for secret note writing!)
- Three Bookmarks
- A "Members Only" Door Hanger
- Two Skeins of J. & P. Coats® Embroidery Floss with flower barrette instruction leaflet
- Two editions of *The Oracle* newsletter
- Plus exclusive Sweet Valley High® product offers, special savings, contests, and much more!

Be the first to find out what Jessica & Elizabeth Wakefield are up to by joining the Sweet Valley High® Fan Club for the one-year membership fee of only $6.25 each for U.S. residents, $8.25 for Canadian residents (U.S. currency). Includes shipping & handling.

Send a check or money order (do not send cash) made payable to "Sweet Valley High® Fan Club" along with this form to:

SWEET VALLEY HIGH® FAN CLUB, BOX 3919-B, SCHAUMBURG, IL 60168-3919

NAME_____
(Please print clearly)

ADDRESS_____

CITY_____ STATE _____ ZIP_____
(Required)

AGE_____ BIRTHDAY_____ /_____ /_____

Offer good while supplies last. Allow 6-8 weeks after check clearance for delivery. Addresses without ZIP codes cannot be honored. Offer good in USA & Canada only. Void where prohibited by law.
©1993 by Francine Pascal   LCI-1383-123